D0467081

The
ROSE AND THE BEAST

FAIRY TALES RETOLD

The
ROSE <small>AND THE</small> BEAST
FAIRY TALES RETOLD

By Francesca Lia Block

JOANNA COTLER BOOKS
An Imprint of HarperCollins*Publishers*

The Rose and the Beast: Fairy Tales Retold
Copyright © 2000 by Francesca Lia Block
For information address HarperCollins Publishers,
1350 Avenue of the Americas, New York, NY 10019.
www.harpercollins.com

Library of Congress Cataloging-in-Publication Data
Block, Francesca Lia.
  The rose and the beast: fairy tales retold / by Francesca Lia
Block.
    p.   cm.
  "Joanna Cotler books."
  Summary: Nine classic fairy tales set in modern, magical
landscapes and retold with a twist.
  ISBN 0-06-028129-4—ISBN 0-06-028130-8 (lib. bdg.)
  [1. Fairy tales.]   I. Title.
PZ8.B6175 Ro 2000   00-22444
[Fic]—dc21   CIP
                                         AC

Typography by Alicia Mikles
1 2 3 4 5 6 7 8 9 10
❖
First Edition

This book is for

my husband, Chris Schuette

With all my love

Snow

Tiny

Glass

Charm

Wolf

Rose

Bones

Beast

Ice

SNOW

When she was born her mother was so young, still a girl herself, didn't know what to do with her. She screamed and screamed—the child. Her mother sat crying in the garden. The gardener came by to dig up the soil. It was winter. The child was frost-colored. The gardener stood before the cold winter sun, blocking the light with his broad shoulders. The mother looked like a broken rose bush.

Take her please, the mother cried. The gardener sat beside her. She was shaking. The child would not stop screaming. When the mother put her in his arms, the child was quiet.

Take her, the mother said. I can't keep her. She will devour me.

The child wrapped her tiny fingers around the gardener's large brown thumb. She stared up at him with her eyes like black rose petals in her snowy face. He said to the mother, Are you sure? And she stood up and ran into the house, sobbing. Are you sure are you sure? She was sure. Take it away, she prayed, it will devour me.

4

The gardener wrapped the child in a clean towel and put her in his truck and drove her west to the canyon. There was no way he could keep her himself, was there? (He imagined her growing up, long and slim, those lips and eyes.) No, but he knew who could.

The seven brothers lived in a house they had built themselves, built deep into the side of the canyon among the trees. They had built it without chopping down one tree, so it was an odd-shaped house with towers and twisting hallways and jagged staircases. It looked like part of the canyon itself, as if it had

5

sprung up there. It smelled of woodsmoke and leaves. From the highest point you could see the sea lilting and shining in the distance.

This was where the gardener brought the child. He knew these men from work they had all done together on a house by the ocean. He was fascinated by the way they worked. They made the gardener feel slow and awkward and much too tall. Also, lonely.

Bear answered the door. Like all the brothers he had a fine, handsome face, burnished skin, huge brown eyes that regarded everyone as if they were the beloved. He was slightly heavier than the others and his hair was soft, thick, close cropped. He shook the gardener's hand and welcomed him inside, politely avoiding the bundle in the gardener's arms until the gardener said, I don't know where to take her.

Bear brought him into the kitchen where Fox, Tiger, and Buck were eating their lunch of vegetable stew and rice, baked apples and blueberry gingerbread. They asked the gardener to join them. When Bear told them why he was there, they allowed themselves to turn their benevolent gazes to the child in his arms. She stared back at them and

the gardener heard an unmistak-
able burbling coo coming from her
mouth.

Buck held her in his muscular
arms. She nestled against him and
closed her eyes—dark lash tassels.
Buck looked down his fine, sculpted
nose at her and whispered, Where
does she come from?

The gardener told him, From the
valley, her mother can't take care of
her. He said he was afraid she would
be hurt if he left her there. The
mother wasn't well. The brothers
gathered around. They knew then
that she was the love they had been
seeking in every face forever before

this. Bear said, We will keep her. And the gardener knew he had done the right thing bringing her here.

The other brothers, Otter, Lynx, and Ram, came home that evening. They also loved her right away, as if they had been waiting forever for her to come. They named her Snow and gave her everything they had.

Bear and Ram built her a room among the trees overlooking the sea. Tiger built her a music-box cradle that rocked and played melodies. Buck sewed her lace dresses and made her tiny boots like the ones he and his brothers wore. They cooked for her—the finest, the healthiest

9

foods, most of which they grew themselves, and she was always surrounded by the flowers Lynx picked from their garden, the candles Fox dipped in the cellar, and the melon-scented soaps that Otter made in his workroom.

She grew up there in the canyon—the only Snow. It was warm in the canyon most days—sometimes winds and rains but never whiteness on the ground. She was their Snow, unbearably white and crystal sweet. She began to grow into a woman and although sometimes this worried them a bit—they were not used to women, especially

10

one like this who was their daughter
and yet not—they learned not to be
afraid, how to show her as much love
as they had when she was a baby and
yet give her a distance that was necessary for them as well as for her. As
they had given her everything, she
gave to them—she learned to hammer
and build, cook, sew, and garden.
She could do anything. They had
given her something else, too—the
belief in herself, instilled by seven
fathers who had had to learn it.
Sometimes at night, gathered around
the long wooden table finishing the
peach-spice or apple-ginger pies and
raspberry tea, they would tell stories

11

of their youth—the things they had suffered separately when they went out alone to try the world. The stories were of freak shows and loneliness and too much liquor or powders and the shame of deformity. They wanted her to know what they had suffered but not to be afraid of it, they wanted her to have everything—the world, too. And to be able to return to them, to safety, whenever she needed. They knew, though, she would not suffer as they had suffered. She was perfect. They were scarred.

She loved them. That is what no one tells. She loved them. They smelled of woodsmoke and sweet earth, where flowers grow. They spoke softly, kindly, sometimes they sang. They were strong and browned from the sun. She believed that they knew everything, could make anything. They loved her as their daughter, sister, mother . . . they loved her. That maybe has been hinted at before, but not that she loved them.

When she was of a certain age the gardener came to visit. He had been reminded of her. The white petals scattering in the garden . . . something, something reminded him, and he came to see what had become of her, if he had been right when he saw her baby face and imagined it grown, and knew he could not keep her.

Lynx looked at him and his eyes were guarded, Lynx's eyes. He did not want to let the gardener in. But he knew, too, this was wrong. The time had come, as they all had known it would. She was a woman now, and restless, and no, they were not her fathers. It was time. So he let the gardener into the house, where she was sitting surrounded by the six other brothers, reading aloud to them. She was wearing a white dress she had made herself, almost as white as her skin, which showed

here and there beneath it, and heavy
black hobnailed boots like the ones
the brothers wore. Her face was
flushed and her eyes burned with
firelight. The gardener wondered,
why had he come here?

She smiled up at him. He was the
first man she'd seen, they kept her so
sheltered. The first man that was not
one of them — a much taller man with
a head more like hers. But he did not
have their eyes or their strong and
lyrical hands.

The gardener was invited to
share in the cherry-mint pie she had
made for the evening, and he spoke
with her, asked about the books she

15

liked to read (they brought her children's stories of magic, and old novels with thick, yellowish pages about passionate women in brutal landscapes) and the music she listened to, did she sew her own dress? She showed him through the night garden she had planted and he knew all about the different bulbs and shrubs, and she liked the way he towered over her and the way his shoulders blocked the moonlight.

The brothers were inside the house trying not to spy, trying to be calm. What could they do? It is time, they told each other.

The gardener left and went back

to the woman with whom he had been
living all these years. The woman who
was Snow's mother. Why had he
gone where he had? He could hardly
look at her. Why had he gone? He
had been right about what that baby
would become. Snow's mother was
crying when he came home, something was wrong, she could tell it,
she could see in his eyes. Something
had died.

No, he thought, something has
been born.

Something had died.

Snow turned over and over in
her bed, her fingers exploring the
palpitations of her body under the

nightdress. She closed her eyes and saw the gardener's dark curls and tall body. But when she dreamed of him, it was a nightmare. He was cutting down trees with an ax and blood ran from their trunks. He was carrying the body of a very pale child into the woods and holding the ax . . .

They tried to console her, seven brothers, as seven fathers would. They tried to be fair; how could they keep her from living her life? Who were they to keep her? They told her that if he came again she could see him but that they didn't want her to be hurt. Maybe there was another man they could find. She didn't know why, but he was the only one—she wanted to speak to him again. Maybe she could sense her mother on his skin. Her mother. She hardly ever asked about this. She assumed she had been lost and they had found her and there was no one. She was her own mother. But oh something else. Breast. Flowers. Silk. Hair. Lavender. Milk. Apple. Blood. Lost.

The woman who was Snow's mother followed the gardener into the canyon one night. She had grown sick with premonitions. She walked around outside the house in the dark, her feet sinking into the damp earth,

19

the crackle of branches, the smell of crushed flowers. Maybe she was looking for what she had lost too. She thought it was the man, but it was more.

Through the window she saw them, the girl and the gardener. The girl was nightmare. Young young young. Silver white. Perfect. Untorn. Perfect.

The gardener was haloed by her light. Dripping her light. After all, she was the baby he had rescued, she might be dead by now if it weren't for him. After all, she was the same flesh as the woman he had made love to for these years. After all, she was young, perfect, untouched. And he had to rescue her from these seven strange, deformed (suddenly he saw them as deformed) men who would suffocate her, make her a freak like they were.

Poison, the mother thought, poison.

And she came back there when the men were away at work, came back with the apples injected with poison. She had read about it — simple recipe — too messy with razor blades. She had thought of using it on herself in the past. Wouldn't this almost be the same thing?

Snow opened the door and love

filled her. She had never seen a woman before. A woman with pale skin and dark hair like hers. Even the redness of the lips and the way the incisors pointed slightly. Something was so familiar that she swooned with it. She had been told not to let strangers in, but this was not a stranger, this was someone she sensed deep in her bones. Like marrow.

The woman said she had brought her a present. Why a present? Your beauty is famous, the woman said. I wanted to honor it. I wanted to see you, too. Some people say we resemble each other.

22

Snow had never thought of herself as beautiful. For her, beauty was Bear's voice telling her bedtime stories and the way Buck's eyes shone and Lynx's small graceful body. She thought it was strange that this woman would want to give her a present because of how she looked.

The brothers had told her not to accept gifts from strangers, but this wasn't a stranger. This was a woman who seemed so familiar. And the apples were so luscious red sleek. They would be hard clean white fresh inside, chilling and sparking her mouth.

23

Snow asked if the woman would like to come in? No no she had to be on her way. She was glad to have seen Snow's face.

The woman hesitated for a moment before she left. She looked sad, Snow thought, or worse—but she wasn't sure what it was, and then the woman was leaving.

Snow went inside and washed the apples and began to cut them up for a pie she would give to the brothers. She felt excited—her heart was pounding and, strangely, she wanted to sing. She hummed the lullaby that her music-box cradle had played when she was a baby, rocking by the

24

fireside while the brothers read aloud or talked softly to her.

A woman had come to her door. There were women out there, in the world. How many of them looked like this one? So like her. They couldn't mostly, could they? Who was this woman? Why had she come? Why did she seem sad and her teeth were sharp. Snow imagined them puncturing the sealed sweet red of the apple skin. She reached down and fingered a slice between her thumb and pointer. The skin was dark dark red like blood. Snow put the piece to her lips and ran her tongue along the ridge. She bit.

They found her lying on the floor with the poison in her veins and the apples spilled where they had rolled. She was the green color of certain white flowers. Each of them tried to expel the poison from her, to breathe life into her. She had a pulse, but hardly—very shallow. They carried her upstairs to the glass bed they had made for her when she outgrew the cradle. When they laid her out in her white dress they wept because without her they knew they would have nothing and their own deaths would come knocking on the door. Seven truncated deaths in fourteen big boots.

My darling, they thought. Sometimes they could not tell if they were
having an individual thought or
sensing each other's. My darling, we
never deserved you. Wake up and
we will let you go into the world
where you belong. This was our
fault, we were wrong to keep you
like this. Don't blame us, though.
Look at our lives before you. Look at
what you gave us.

They called the gardener.

When the gardener came they
let him go to her alone. They sat
downstairs in the dim—just a single
candle—working on the gifts they

would give to her if only she woke. These gifts she would take into the world—dresses of silk, necklaces of glass beads and shells, glass candlesticks and champagne glasses and tiny glass animals, candles and incense and bath salts and soaps and quilts and coverlets and a miniature house with a real garden and tiny fountains that she could keep at her bedside.

The gardener went to her and held her hand. It felt like it would slip away, it was so thin and light; it felt boneless. The gardener said he was going to take her away with him, help her get better. Why was he hesitating? He wanted to look at her like this, for a while. He wanted this stillness. She was completely his, now, in a way she would never be again. His silent, perfect bride. Not like the woman who had come screaming to him—what have I done? He brushed the dark, damp strands of hair off her smooth forehead. He leaned close to her, breathing her like one would inhale a bouquet. He looked at her lips, half parted as if waiting for him. He wanted to possess.

But when he touched her with his mouth and her eyes opened she did not see him there. She called for

29

the men, the seven brothers. She wanted them. More than gardeners or mothers. She wanted them the way she needed the earth and the flowers and the sky and the sea from her tower room and food and sleep and warmth and light and nights by the fire and poetry and the stories of going out into the world and almost being destroyed by it and returning to find comfort and the real meaning of freak. And I am a freak, she thought, happily. I am meant to stay here forever. I am loved.

She pushed the gardener away and called for them. In her sleep she had seen love. It was poisoning. It was possessing. Devouring. Or it was seven pairs of boots climbing up the stairs to find her.

TINY

he woman named her lost babies Berry, Ivy, Oxygen, Pie, Whistler, Willow, Wish, and Pear, never knowing if they were boys or girls. Each one taught her something about life. Sorrow, Pain, Fortitude, Tenderness, Patience, Courage, Awe, Love. She made eight tiny symbolic graves in her garden and planted flowers on them all.

The woman sat alone in her

garden of memory flowers, rocking a cradle full of iris bulbs, whispering to babies who could not hear her. She felt like the ancient cracking husk of a pomegranate, rattling with dried seeds.

And then she found she was pregnant again.

The doctors were amazed because the fetus was much too small, but this time there was a perfectly normal heartbeat flickering on the screen like a miniature star.

The woman prayed to the spirits of the lost babies that this one would come out all right.

And it did. Except that the baby

36

was tiny, just about the size of a thumb. Her mother called her Tiny. You are perfect, the mother told her, the baby I always wanted. She was careful to make sure her child did not feel sad because of her small size.

Tiny had to sleep in a cradle made from half a walnut shell and drink out of a thimble. Even dollhouse doll clothes were too big for her, so mostly she ran around naked or clothed in scraps of silk.

Tiny didn't know there was anything wrong with her for a long time. She loved her mother and thought all mothers were big like that. She believed that when she was older she might suddenly grow and one day have a child the size of her own thumb. Her life was happy. She sat on the edge of the flower box filled with red, white, and magenta impatiens and watched the garden bloom. She could see the most infinitesimal movements of the plants as they grew. It was enough to occupy her all day, that and being with her mother. She could gaze at her mother forever as if her mother were a lush and flowering plant towering above all the rest.

Tiny was protected from the outside world in the gated garden full of roses, irises, and azaleas, orange, lemon, and avocado trees, and she didn't mind. The garden got more radiant and abundant and redolent every day that she watched it and, as her mother said, blessed it, although she didn't know how she did that, really. She had so much going on inside her head—so many things to dream about. She had eight imaginary playmates that came to her and taught her things about life. About how sad life is, but also how full of wonder, and about being strong and letting go and believing that things will bloom again. Tiny was fine in her tiny world. But one day she saw the boy.

39

He had climbed over the garden fence because he had heard that the woman with the long legs and the cat eyes lived in that shady, fragrant home. She didn't come out much anymore, people said. The tragedy of her life. They didn't know about her tiny secret.

Tiny saw the boy wandering around the garden, as intrigued by the flowers as she was, it seemed. It was true, he'd never seen a garden like this one before. The blossoms were huge and the fragrance was staggering. He felt drunk.

He was tall and thin with a long face and deep-set eyes with heavy

40

brows. He was not particularly good looking—at least he didn't think so. He felt ungainly tripping on his big feet as if to escape his body—cumbersome. But to Tiny he was wonderful. Full of wonder. Terrifying. He was everything she wanted. She stopped caring about the garden and the eight spirit babies who visited her, and even about her mother. Suddenly she resented her mother a little, without quite recognizing the emotion since it was so new to her, but felt it because she realized in that instant that she would never be tall and big like that; she was a freak, she knew, and this boy would never love her.

41

The boy prowled around the garden, dizzy with the flowers. He was a poet and was already thinking of words to try to describe what he saw (he couldn't). He peeked into the windows of the house and saw the woman walking around with her hair up in a turban towel. She was about his mother's age but she had long legs, high cheekbones, and the upward-slanting sun-flecked green eyes of a cat.

Tiny saw him watching. She needed to scream but she just lay there, oozing and broken like a squashed insect.

The boy waited while Tiny's

42

mother loosened the towel from her head so that her long wet hair shook down. He waited while she let her robe slip from her shoulders. Tiny came closer to him. She could hear his breathing, raspy and deep in his throat, and she could smell something that was better than all the flowers in her garden.

The boy suddenly swung around, sensing, but not seeing anyone. He ran out of the garden.

Tiny thought about him every day and night. She became sullen and would hardly speak or eat. Her mother asked her again and again what was wrong but she wouldn't say. Her eyes became like slits and she chewed on her lips until they bled. She felt like the dead butterfly she had seen moldering in the dirt.

Tiny knew it was time to leave and so she packed up some berries, her bed linens, her thimble, and a silver needle in a knapsack and began her journey away from the garden and from the mother whom she would never be.

If you were Tiny's size you would find that a few blocks can take a long long time to traverse. There were many dangers. The bird that swooped down and tried to eat her for lunch. The toad that fell in

love with her and tried to carry her
away to be its wife. The cat that
thought she was a toy to bat around
in its claws. With her silver needle
and her quick little body, Tiny was
able to get away. She was no longer
a slow dreamer watching the flowers grow. She was a warrior now.
Warriors need something to fight for,
though, besides their lives, because
otherwise their lives will not be
worth it. Tiny thought she was fighting for the boy's love, but after a
while she wondered what that meant
and how did she think she could ever
achieve it? Small as she was—the
size of one of his fingers—nothing

45

like her mother, with nothing to give except a way to watch gardens, some knowledge imparted by eight spirit babies, now gone, and deftness with a silver needle.

The boy was walking home from school trying to find words to describe the way he was feeling. Alone, awkward, alienated, isolated, crazy. He hated all those words. He wondered why he considered himself a poet. Pretentious as hell. He thought everything he wrote was terrible, actually. He had tried to write about the garden, and the woman in the window, and the strange feeling

46

he had had, as if he were being
watched, breathed upon by something that chilled his nape and made
him want to cry.

Tiny found him that day. She was
half starved. She had been scratched
and bitten. Her dress was in tatters.
Not one night had she slept well —
there was no safe garden, no walnut
cradle, no lullaby mother. She was
too old for these things anyway, she
told herself. Tinys do not deserve
safety. If they are to prove themselves, they must suffer and die or
suffer and survive.

But then she saw the boy, and
love seeped into her body as if she

47

had sucked it from a honeysuckle blossom. She knew he was trying to make up poems. She knew so much about him already. She realized that she was nothing without his desire for poetry, just as she was nothing without her mother's desire for a child. She was their creation; no wonder she had to have them.

This made her feel strangely brave and she leaped as far as she could, landing precariously on his arm. His jacket smelled of smoke and basketball and libraries and the grass he had rolled in, trying to recall what it was like when he was a little boy and not so . . . whatever it was that he was all the time. Sad, depressed, angst-ridden. He didn't even have the right words left for anything.

Tiny jumped from his scratchy sleeve into his pocket, where it was warm and musty smelling. There was a pack of cigarettes, a gnawed pencil stub, some grains of sand, a piece of spearmint gum in case he ever met who he was waiting for. She explored, discovering new things about him. How he worried about lung cancer but couldn't stop smoking. How he always lay on the beach in his clothes, wishing the ocean would take him away, he didn't care where. How he was waiting for his muse, his

49

poetry in the shape of a girl.

And so Tiny waited also, and when he came to his apartment building and went inside, and closed the door of his room that was piled with books replacing tables and chairs and had black-and-white posters from Italian movies on the walls (all the women were so big like Tiny's mother), and had a rumpled bed with sheets like maps—that was when she climbed out of his pocket and stood in front of him. Now she was truly a warrior because he was a million times more dangerous to her than toads, cats, or birds.

Oh, shit, he said. What the fuck.

50

I'm Tiny, she said.

You can say that again.

I'm Tiny.

He laughed. Man! he said. You are awe-inspiring, O Muse.

I've been trying to find you, she said.

Well, Tiny Muse, I'm certainly glad that you have.

He got down on his knees before her—she was perched on a stack of books of Beat poetry—and stared at every part of her perfect little body. He felt a bit perverse about it, but he didn't care because she seemed to be enjoying his gaze. He knew that he would never be without the right words again as long as she was with him, but he thought he should officially ask her anyway.

Will you help me to find the words, O Muse? he asked.

She looked him up and down, looked around the room.

Can I sleep in your bed? she answered.

He grinned at her and reached for the piece of gum in his pocket.

Suddenly he was translucent, perfect, the size she was.

The prince of the flowers.

GLASS

She did not mind her days alone, away from the eyes outside. It was better this way, her secret stories hidden so no one could touch them, take them. Her sisters listened, rapt, but did not try to take. They cared more for the eyes and ears; they seemed to want to collect these like charms to wear around their necks, the eyes and ears and the mouths whispering—beautiful, beautiful, why did it matter she wondered. She was free, still, like a child, the way it is before you are seen and then after that you can never remember who you are unless someone else shows it to you. She had the stories she gave to her sisters that made them love her. Or need her, at least.

And she had the tasks. She loved to plant the beds with lilies and wisteria, camellias and gardenias, until her hands were caked with earth. To arrange the flowers in the vase like dancing sisters. To make the salmon in pomegranate sauce; the salads of spinach, red onion, pine nuts, oranges, and avocados; the golden

vanilla cream custards; the breads
and piecrusts that powdered her
with flour. She loved, even, to dust
the things, to feel them in her hands,
imagining their history. The glass
music box that perhaps a boy had
once given to his grandparents—the
first present he had ever chosen,
making them close their eyes, watching them standing there, before him,
suddenly looking so small with their
eyelids closed and their hands held
out until they heard the tinkle of
their first dance. The glass goblet
with the roses and grape clusters one
could feel with the fingertips like
Braille that perhaps a man had given

57

to his wife because she was losing her sight and he was afraid to give her more books of poetry. The candlesticks like crystal balls, many-faceted; though the girl could not read her own future in them perhaps if she looked closely enough she could see the young bride tearing away the tissue and holding them up to the light to see herself being imagined by this girl, now. This girl, now, who did not mind polishing the wooden floors or scrubbing out the pots until her sisters could see their reflections, or cleaning between the tiles and lighting the candles, running the water and scattering the petals and powders in the bath so that her sisters could lie in the tub where she would tell them stories. Always she would tell them stories; they returned at night and sat before their mirrors, let her rub their feet with almond oil, soothe them with her words and in this way she felt loved.

But the woman came to her then. The woman with hair of red like roses, hair of white like snowfall. She was young and old. She was blind and could see everything. She spoke softly, in whispers, but her voice carried across the mountain ranges like sleeping giants, the cities lit like fairies and the oceans—undulating mermaids. She laughed at her own sorrow and wept pearls at weddings. Her fingers were branches and her eyes were little blue planets. She said, You cannot hide forever, though you may try. I've seen you in the kitchen, in the garden. I've seen the things you have sewn—curtains of dawn, twilight blankets and dresses for the sisters like a garden of stars. I have heard the stories you tell. You are the one who transforms, who creates. You can go out into the world and show others. They will feel less alone because of you, they will feel understood, unburdened by

you, awakened by you, freed of guilt
and shame and sorrow. But to share
with them you must wear shoes you
must go out you must not hide
you must dance and it will be harder
you must face jealousy and sometimes rage and desire and love which
can hurt most of all because of what
can then be taken away. So make
that astral dress to fit your own body
this time. And here are glass shoes
made from your words, the stories
you have told like a blower with her
torch forming the thinnest, most
translucent sheets of light out of
what was once sand. But be careful;
sand is already broken but glass

breaks. The shoes are for dancing not for running away.

So she washed off the dust and ash and flour and mud and went to the dance where sure enough everyone whirled around her, entranced by the stories in which they recognized themselves, but in the stories they were also more than themselves and it always felt at the end fulfilled not meaningless and empty like life can sometimes feel. She knew they all loved her with her stories because they became her and she became them.

He came to her across the marble floor, past the tall windows glowing

like candles, the balconies overlooking the reflecting pools full of swans,
the stone statues of goddesses and
beds of heady roses—had she made
all of this, like a story? He had dense
curls and soft full lips and bright
eyes like a woodland beast and a
body of lithe muscle and mostly she
could see he was gentle, he was
gentle like a boy though he could lift
her in his hands. He held her and she
felt his hard chest and stomach and
hipbones and she felt his strong
heart beating like the sound of all the
stories she could ever hope to tell.
Maybe she had not created him,
maybe she was his creation and all

she dreamed, his dream. Or maybe they had made each other. Yes.

Beloved. One. He planted in her a seed of a white flower with a dizzy scent; in the night garden the oranges hung like fat moonstruck jewels and the jasmine bloomed as she spun and spun. Now she had everything and the sisters eyed her jealously, secretly, in their mirrors until the glass cracked, clutched the little bags she had made for them until the crystal beads scattered and broke—they had stories, too, they'd like to tell. They'd like to make someone cry and swoon and spin with love for what they made. Who was she to take this away from them? How dare she wear the glass shoes? They could see what was wrong with her. She wasn't perfect, she wasn't so beautiful. Her skin was blemished and her body was too thin, or not thin enough, and she wasn't perfectly symmetrical and her hair was thin and brittle and why was he looking at her like that? It was just that she knew how to make things. Or not even that—just rearrange, imitate.

She felt their envy and this broke her. The story ended, she couldn't tell the rest, they'd hate her, she had to stop it, she wasn't any good shut up you bad bad girl ugly and you don't deserve any of this and so the spell was broken and she ran home through a tangle of words where the letters jumbled and made no sense and meant nothing, and the words were ugly and she was not to be heard or seen, she was blemished and too fat, too thin, not smart, too smart, not good, not a storyteller, not a creator, not beautiful, not a woman not not not. All the things that girls feel they are not when they fear that if they become, if they are, they will no longer be loved by the sisters whose hearts they have not meant to break. And besides, if the sisters are gone and only the beloved remains

66

with his dense curls and his lips, how safe are you then? You have to have him or you will die if the sisters are gone with their listening ears and their feet to rub and their bodies to dress and their shared loneliness.

She lost one of the glass slippers — shine, fire, bright of her making like a dropped word lost, like a word, the missing word to make the story right again, to make it complete.

It doesn't matter, she tells herself, shredding up the dress she made. It doesn't matter, I am safe. Alone and safe. The sisters don't hate me. I am small and safe, no one will hate me, hear me, no one can break me by leaving, by taking away his seed, the promise of the jasmine blossom in the garden.

Still he came to find her even without her enchantments, her stories, her dress, her shoe. He had the shoe, he'd found it when he followed her. It was so fragile he didn't breathe.

She made him want to cry when he walked up the path through the ferns and doves and lilies and saw her covered with earth and dust and ash. Only her eyes shone out. Revealing, not reflecting. Windows. Her feet were bare. He wanted her to tell him the rest of the story. He

felt bereft without it, without her.
There were only these women with
mirror eyes strutting across marble
floors, tossing their manes, revealing
their breasts, untouchable, only
these tantalizing empty glass boxes
full of dancing lights he could not
hold, only these icy cubicles, parched
yards, hard loneliness.

When the sisters saw him kneel-
ing before her holding the one shoe,
not breathing, trying not to crush
anything, saw how he looked at her,
how he needed her, they knew that if
they tried to take this from her they
would never know, have nothing left,
they would starve, they would break,

69

they would never wake up.

The fairy who was not old, not young, who was red roses, white snowfall, who was blind and saw everything, who sent stories resounding through the universe said, You must reach inside yourselves where I live like a story, not old, not young, laughing at my own sorrow, weeping pearls at weddings, wielding a torch to melt sand into something clear and bright.

CHARM

he felt like the girl in the fairy tale. Maybe there had been some kind of curse. Inevitable that she would prick her arm (not her finger) with the needle. Did the girl feel this ecstasy of pure honeyed light in her veins, like being infused with the soul she had lost? For Rev, that was all there was.

The flood was like an ogre's tears. Mud and trees and even small children were carried away in it. Rev's vintage Thunderbird was swept down the canyon, landing crashed at the bottom, full of water and leaves.

Fires like dragon's breath consumed the poppies and lupine, the jacaranda trees that once flowered purple in sudden overnight bursts of exuberance as if startled at their own capacity for gorgeousness.

When the earth quaked, the walls of Rev's house cracked; all the glasses and teacups in her cabinet careened out, covering the floor in a sharp carpet that cut her feet as she ran outside. Chimneys and windows

74

wailed. Rev was amazed at how, with
the power all out, she could see the
stars above her, clearly, for the first
time since she was a child on a camp-
ing trip in the desert. They were like
the glass fragments on the floor. The
air smelled of leaking gas. Her feet
were bleeding into the damp lawn.

This is my city, Rev thought.
Cursed, like I am cursed. Sleeping,
like I sleep. Tear-flooded and fever-
scorched, quaking and bloodied with
nightmares.

She went out in the city with its
lights like a radioactive phosphores-
cence, wandered through galleries
where the high-priced art on the

walls was the same as the graffiti scrawled outside by taggers who were arrested or killed for it, went to parties in hotel rooms where white-skinned, lingerie-clad rock stars had been staying the night their husbands shot themselves in the head, listened to music in nightclubs where stunning boyish actors had OD'd on the pavement. When the sun began to come up Rev went back to her canyon house where vines had begun to grow through the cracks in the walls. The air smelled acrid and stale—eucalyptus and cigarettes. Her television was always on.

Pop came by in his dark glasses,

leather pants, and long blond dread-
locks. He gave her what she needed
in a needle in exchange for the pho-
tos he took of her. And sometimes
she slept with him.

Sleeping Beauty, he said. I like
you this way.

She was wearing her kimono
with the embroidered red roses, her
hair in her face. Hipbones haunting
through silk and flesh.

You have opium eyes.

Opium eyes. She closed her heavy
lids over them, wanting to sleep.

He photographed her as witch,
priestess, fairy queen, garden. He
photographed her at the ruins of the

castle and on the peeling, mournful carousel and in the fountain.

It's like you're from nowhere, Pop said. I like that. It's like you live inside my head. I made you just the way I wanted you to be.

Where am I from? she wondered. Maybe Pop was right. She was only in his head. But there had been something before.

She had been adopted by a man and a woman who wanted beauty. The woman thought of champagne roses, rose champagne, perfume, and jewels, but she couldn't have a child. The child they found was darker than they had hoped for but even more lavishly numinous. They had men take pictures of her right from the beginning. There were things that happened. Rev tried to think only of the leopard couches and velvet pillows, the feather boas and fox fur pelts, the flock of doves and the poodle with its forelock twisted into a unicorn horn, the hot lights that were, she hoped, bright enough to sear away the image of what was happening to her. She could not, though she tried, remember the face of the other girl who had been there once.

Was the curse that she was born too beautiful? Had it caused her real parents to abandon her, fearful of the length of lash, the plush of lip in such a young face? Was it the reason the men with cameras had sucked away her soul in little sips, because any form that lovely must remain soulless so as not to stun them impotent? Was it what made Old-Woman-Heroin's face split into a jealous leer as she beckoned Rev up to the attic and stabbed her with the needle that first time?

Because she no longer had a car, she let Pop drive her around. He picked her up one night and took her to a small white villa. It belonged to an actress named Miss Charm. Pop led Rev upstairs, past the sleek smoky people drinking punch out of an aquarium and into a room that was painted to look like a shell. He told her to take off her dress and arranged her limbs on a big white bed, tied and slapped her arm, tucked the needle into the largest, least bruised vein. Then the three men climbed onto her while Pop hovered around them snapping shots. Rev did not cry out. She lay still. She let the opium be her soul. It was better than having a soul. It did not cry out, it did not writhe with pain.

Get off of her, you fucks! a voice screamed like the soul Rev no longer had.

81

The young woman had shorn black hair and pale skin.

Get out of my house, she said.

Oh chill, Charm.

Leave now, she said.

Want to join the party? one of the men said. I think she wants to join the party.

Rev felt her empty insides trying to jump out of her as if to prove there was no soul there, nothing anyone had to be afraid of, nothing left for them to want to have. She felt her emptiness bitter and burning coming up from her throat. The other woman held up a small sharp kitchen knife and the men moved away.

The pale woman helped Rev to
the bathroom and wiped her face
with a warm wet towel. Rev looked
at her reflection in the mirror. She
had shadows underneath her eyes as
if her makeup had been put on
upside down. But in spite of that,
nothing had changed. She still bore
the curse.

You're going to be okay, the
woman was saying in a hard voice
like: you have to be.

Rev stared at her.

I know, the woman said.

She ran a bath for Rev and lit the
candles that were arranged around the
tub like torches along the ramparts of

a castle. She filled the water with oils that smelled like the bark, leaves, and blossoms of trees from a sacred grove. The mirrors blurred with steam like a mystic fog so that Rev could not see her own image. She was thankful.

While Rev bathed, the woman stripped off the sheets from the white bed and bleached and boiled them clean. She opened all the windows that looked out over the courtyard full of banana trees, Chinese magnolia, bird of paradise, and hibiscus flowers. She lit incense in sconces all around the room and played a tape of Tibetan monks chanting.

84

Rev got out of the bath and dried herself off with the clean white towel the woman had left for her. She put on the heavy clean white robe that had been stolen from some fancy hotel and walked barefoot into the bedroom.

Are you hungry? the woman asked.

Rev shook her head.

Do you want to sleep here tonight?

Rev nodded. Sleep sleep sleep. That was what she wanted.

She woke the next night. The woman was sitting at her bedside with a silver tray. She had made a meal of jasmine rice, coconut milk, fresh mint, and chiles. There were tall glasses of mineral water with slices of lime like green moons rising above clear bubbling pools. There was a glass bowl full of gardenias.

Can you eat now? There was an expression on the woman's face that seemed vaguely familiar. Rev thought of how her adopted mother's face had looked when she would not get out of bed after something had happened with the photographer. No, it was not that. Maybe she was remembering another woman, before that one. A woman with eyes that were always wet.

I thought I forgot her, Rev said. My real mother. You remind me of her.

How?

Because of your eyes now.

What happened? Why was she crying?

I used to think she gave me up because I was cursed.

Cursed? the woman said.

Rev looked down and pulled the blankets up over her heavy, satiny breasts.

Blessed, said the woman. She was crying because you are blessed and because she had to give you up.

The woman was wearing a white

men's T-shirt. Her face was scrubbed clean of makeup. Her cheekbones were almost equine. She had a few freckles over the bridge of her nose. Eat something now, she said.

Rev found, strangely, that she was hungry. She ate the sweet and spicy, creamy minty rice and drank the fizzing lime-stung mineral water. She breathed the gardenias. She watched the woman's eyes. They were like the eyes of old-time movie stars, always lambent, making the celluloid look slicked with water, lit with candles.

You can stay here as long as you need to, the woman said.

But I'm going to need . . . Rev began.

If you need it I'll get it for you. Until you decide you want to stop. I stopped.

Rev nodded. Her hair fell forward over her face.

If you need me I'll be sleeping in the next room, said the woman.

But this is your bed, said Rev.

It's yours for now.

She stroked Rev's hand.

Rev slept for days and days. Sometimes she woke kicking her legs and feet until the comforter slid from the bed. Then she would feel someone covering her with satin and

down again, touching her clammy
forehead with dry, soft, gardenia-
scented fingertips. Sometimes she
woke shivering, sweating, quaking
or parched. Always the hands would
be there to warm or cool or still her,
to hold a shimmering glass of water
to her cracking lips.

Sometimes Rev dreamed she was
in a garden gathering flowers that bit
at her hands with venemous mouths.
She dreamed she was running from
creatures who bared needles instead
of teeth. One of them caught her and
pierced her neck. She was falling
falling down a spiral staircase into
darkness. She was lying in a coffin

that was a castle, suffocating under roses. A woman came and knelt beside her, to stitch up her wounds with a silver needle and golden thread.

One night Rev heard, through the mother-of-pearl-painted walls, the soft, muffled animal sounds of someone crying. She got out of bed like a sleepwalker. The night was warm and soft on her bare skin. It clothed her like the robe the princess had dreamed of spinning when she found the old woman in the attic—a fabric of gold filigree lace. How many years the princess had dreamed of spinning such a garment.

91

But there were never any spinning wheels to be found in the whole kingdom. And then, finally, when her chance had come to ornament her beauty the way she wished, for the imagined forbidden lover with the small high breasts and sweet, wet hair and gentle eyes, she had pricked herself and fallen into the death sleep.

Perhaps it was what she deserved for wanting to make herself more beautiful. And for wanting what she could not have.

Rev went out the bedroom door and into the hall. The house was dark and silent except for the sound of muffled weeping.

In the room where the woman lay it was darker still. Rev found her way to the bed by sound and touch. Her hands caught onto something warm and curved and fragile-feeling. It was the woman's hipbone jutting out from beneath the blankets.

Why are you crying? Rev asked. Her hand slid down over the hipbone, across the woman's taut abdomen working with sobs.

The woman reached for a silk tassel and pulled the embroidered piano-shawl curtains back. Moonlight flooded the room. She handed Rev a small battered black-and-white photograph.

Do you remember? the woman asked.

Rev stared at the two naked young girls, one dark, one pale, curled on a leopard-skin sofa. Their hands and feet were shackled together. It was herself and the woman. That was why the eyes had looked familiar.

My stepfather took this, the woman said.

These two girls. Only with each other were they young. They would take each other's hands and run screaming through the night. No one could touch them, then. Dressed as ragged, raging boys; people were afraid of them. Devouring stolen roses and gardenias, stuffing their faces with petals. Rolling in the dirt, scratching so that their nails ached, filled with soil. The fair-skinned one would bind the other's breasts, gently, gently, so they were hidden away in the flannel shirt. The dark-skinned one would wipe the powder and paint from the other's face. They would trace each other's initials with a razor blade on their palms and hold hands till their blood was one. These secret rampages were their own—they could look at each other anywhere, no matter what was happening around them—to them—and be free, be back, roaming, hollering, shrieking, untouched except by each other.

Charm, Rev said. Miss Charm.

I shouldn't have asked you to stay, said Charm. I shouldn't have made you remember.

I'll go then, Rev said. If you want.

I don't want you to go, Charm whispered. I've been waiting for you so long. Her voice reminded Rev of a piece of broken jewelry.

I thought he had taken my soul, said Rev.

I thought he took mine, too. But no one can. It's just been sleeping.

When Charm kissed her, Rev felt as if all the fierce blossoms were shuddering open. The castle was opening. She felt as if the other woman were breathing into her body something long lost and almost forgotten. It was, she knew, the only drug either of them would need now.

WOLF

They don't believe me. They think I'm crazy. But let me tell you something it be a wicked wicked world out there if you didn't already know.

My mom and he were fighting and that was nothing new. And he was drinking, same old thing. But then I heard her mention me, how she knew what he was doing. And no fucking way was she going to sit around and let that happen. She was taking me away and he better not try to stop her. He said, no way, she couldn't leave.

That's when I started getting scared for both of us, my mom and me. How the hell did she know about that? He would think for sure I told her. And then he'd do what he had promised he'd do every night he held me under the crush of his putrid skanky body.

I knew I had to get out of there. I put all my stuff together as quick and quiet as possible—just some clothes, and this one stuffed lamb my mom gave me when I was little and my piggy-bank money that I'd been saving—and I climbed out the window of the condo. It was a hot night and I could smell my own sweat but it was different. I smelled the same old fear I'm used to but it was mixed with the night and the air and the moon and the trees and it was like freedom, that's what I smelled on my skin.

Same old boring boring story America can't stop telling itself. What is this sicko fascination? Every book and movie practically has to have a little, right? But why do you think all those runaways are on the streets tearing up their veins with junk and selling themselves so they can sleep in the gutter? What do you think the alternative was at home?

I booked because I am not a victim by nature. I had been planning on leaving, but I didn't want to lose my mom and I knew the only way I could get her to leave him was if I told her what he did. That was out of the question, not only because of what he might do to me but what it would do to her.

I knew I had to go back and help her, but I have to admit to you that at that moment I was scared shitless and it didn't seem like the time to try any heroics. That's when I knew I had to get to the desert because there was only one person I had in the world besides my mom.

I really love my mom. You know we were like best friends and I didn't even really need any other friend. She was so much fun to hang with. We cut each other's hair and shared clothes. Her taste was kind of youngish and cute, but it worked because she looked pretty young. People thought we were sisters. She knew all the song lyrics and we sang along in the car. We both can't carry a tune. Couldn't? What else about her? It's so hard to think of things sometimes, when you're trying to describe somebody so someone else will know. But that's the thing about it—no one can ever know. Basically you're totally alone and the only person in the world who made me feel not completely that way was her because after all we were made of the same stuff. She used to say to me, Baby, I'll always be with you. No matter what happens to me I'm still here. I believed her until he started coming into my room. Maybe she was still with me but I couldn't be with her those times. It was like if I did then she'd hurt so bad I'd lose her forever.

I figured the only place I could go would be to the desert, so I got together all my money and went to the bus station and bought a ticket. On the ride I started getting the shakes real bad thinking that maybe I shouldn't have left my mom alone like that and maybe I should go back but I was chickenshit, I guess. I leaned my head on the glass and it felt cool and when we got out of the city I started feeling a little better like I could breathe. L.A. isn't really so bad as people think. I guess. I mean there are gangs at my school but they aren't really active or violent except for the isolated incident. I have experienced one big earthquake in my life and it really didn't bother me so much because I'd rather feel out of control at the mercy of nature than other ways, if you know what I mean. I just closed my eyes and let it ride itself out. I kind of wished he'd been on top of me then because it might have scared him and made him feel retribution was at hand, but I seriously doubt that. I don't blame the earth for shaking because she is probably so sick of people fucking with her all the time—building things and poisoning her and that. L.A. is also known for the smog, but my mom said that when she was growing up it was way worse and that they had to have smog alerts all the time where they couldn't do P.E. Now that part I would have liked because P.E. sucks. I'm not very athletic, maybe 'cause I smoke, and I hate getting undressed in front of some of those stupid bitches who like to see what kind of underwear you have on so they can dis you in yet another ingenious way. Anyway, my smoking is way worse for my lungs than the smog, so I don't care about it too much. My mom hated that I smoke and she tried everything— tears and the patch and Nicorette and homeopathic remedies and trips to an acupuncturist, but finally she gave up.

I was wanting a cigarette bad on that bus and thinking about how it would taste, better than the normal taste in my mouth, which I consider tainted by him, and how I can always weirdly breathe a lot better when I have one. My mom read somewhere that smokers smoke as a way to breathe more, so yoga is supposed to help, but that is one thing she couldn't get me to try. My grandmother, I knew she wouldn't mind the smoking—what could she say? My mom called her Barb the chimney. There is something so dry and brittle, so sort of flammable about her, you'd think it'd be dangerous for her to light up like that.

I liked the desert from when I visited there. I liked that it was hot and clean-feeling, and the sand and rocks and cactus didn't make you think too much about love and if you had it or not. They kind of made your mind still, whereas L.A. — even the best parts, maybe especially the best parts, like flowering trees and neon signs and different kinds of ethnic food and music — made you feel agitated and like you were never really getting what you needed. Maybe L.A. had some untapped resources and hidden treasures that would make me feel full and happy and that I didn't know about yet but I wasn't dying to find them just then. If I had a choice I'd probably like to go to Bali or someplace like that where people are more natural and believe in art and dreams and color and love. Does any place like that exist? The main reason L.A. was okay was because that is where my mom was and anywhere she was I had decided to make my home.

On the bus there was this boy with straight brown hair hanging in his pale freckled face. He looked really sad. I wanted to talk to him so much but of course I didn't. I am freaked that if I get close to a boy he will somehow find out what happened to me — like it's a scar he'll see or a smell or something, a red flag — and he'll hate me and go away. This boy kind of looked like maybe something had happened to him, too, but you can't know for sure. Sometimes I'd think I'd see signs of it in people but then I wondered if I was just trying not to feel so alone. That sounds sick, I guess, trying to almost wish what I went through on someone else for company. But I don't mean it that way. I don't wish it on anyone, believe me, but if they've been there I would like to talk to them about it.

The boy was writing furiously in a notebook, like maybe a journal, which I thought was cool. This journal now is the best thing I've ever done in my whole life. It's the only good thing really that they've given me here.

One of our assignments was to write about your perfect dream day. I wonder what this boy's perfect dream day would be. Probably to get to fuck Pamela Lee or something. Unless he was really as cool as I hoped, in which case it would be to wake up in a bed full of cute kitties and puppies and eat a bowl full of chocolate chip cookies in milk and

114

get on a plane and get to go to a
warm, clean, safe place (the cats and
dogs would arrive there later, not
at all stressed from their journey)
where you could swim in blue-crystal
water all day naked without being
afraid and you could lie in the sun
and tell your best friend (who was
also there) your funniest stories so
that you both laughed so hard you
thought you'd pop and at night
you got to go to a restaurant full
of balloons and candles and stuffed
bears, like my birthdays when I was
little, and eat mounds of ice cream
after removing the circuses of tiny
plastic animals from on top.

In my case, the best friend would be my mom, of course, and maybe this boy if he turned out to be real cool and not stupid.

I fell asleep for a little while and I had this really bad dream. I can't remember what it was but I woke up feeling like someone had been slugging me. And then I thought about my mom, I waited to feel her there with me, like I did whenever I was scared, but it was like those times when he came into my room—she wasn't anywhere. She was gone then and I think that was when I knew but I wouldn't let myself.

I think when you are born an

116

angel should say to you, hopefully kindly and not in the fake voice of an airline attendant: Here you go on this long, long dream. Don't even try to wake up. Just let it go on until it is over. You will learn many things. Just relax and observe because there just is pain and that's it mostly and you aren't going to be able to escape no matter what. Eventually it will all be over anyway. Good luck.

I had to get off the bus before the boy with the notebook and as I passed him he looked up. I saw in his journal that he hadn't been writing but sketching, and he ripped out a page and handed it to me. I saw it was a picture of a girl's face but that is all that registered because I was thinking about how my stomach had dropped, how I had to keep walking, step by step, and get off the bus and I'd never be able to see him again and somehow it really really mattered.

When I got off the bus and lit up I saw that the picture was me—except way prettier than I think I look, but just as sad as I feel. And then it was too late to do anything because the bus was gone and so was he.

I stopped at the liquor store and bought a bag of pretzels and a Mountain Dew because I hadn't eaten all day and my stomach was talking pretty loud. Everything tasted of bitter smoke. Then after I'd eaten I started walking along the road to my grandma's. She lives off the highway on this dirt road surrounded by cactus and other desert plants. It was pretty dark so you could see the stars really big and bright, and I thought how cold the sky was and not welcoming or magical at all. It just made me feel really lonely. A bat flew past like a sharp shadow and I could hear owls and coyotes. The coyote howls were the sound I would have made if I could have. Deep and sad but scary enough that

119

no one would mess with me, either.

My grandma has a used stuff store so her house is like this crazy warehouse full of junk like those little plaster statuettes from the seventies of these ugly little kids with stupid sayings that are supposed to be funny, and lots of old clothes like army jackets and jeans and ladies' nylon shirts, and cocktail glasses, broken china, old books, trinkets, gadgets, just a lot of stuff that you think no one would want but they do, I guess, because she's been in business a long time. Mostly people come just to talk to her because she is sort of this wise woman of the desert who's been through a lot in her life and then they end up buying something, I think, as a way to pay her back for the free counseling. She's cool, with a desert-lined face and a bandanna over her hair and long skinny legs in jeans. She was always after my mom to drop that guy and move out here with her but my mom wouldn't. My mom still was holding on to her secret dream of being an actress but nothing had panned out yet. She was so pretty, I thought it would, though. Even though she had started to look a little older. But she could have gotten those commercials where they use

121

the women her age to sell household products and aspirin and stuff. She would have been good at that because of her face and her voice, which are kind and honest and you just trust her.

I hadn't told Grandma anything about him, but I think she knew that he was fucked up. She didn't know how much, though, or she wouldn't have let us stay there. Sometimes I wanted to go and tell her, but I was afraid then Mom would have to know and maybe hate me so much that she'd kick me out.

My mom and I used to get dressed up and put makeup on each

other and pretend to do commercials. We had this mother-daughter one that was pretty cool. She said I was a natural, but I wouldn't want to be an actor because I didn't like people looking at me that much. Except that boy on the bus, because his drawing wasn't about the outside of my body, but how I felt inside and you could tell by the way he did it, and the way he smiled, that he understood those feelings so I didn't mind that he saw them. My mom felt that I'd be good anyway, because she said that a lot of actors don't like people looking at them and that is how they create these personas to

123

hide behind so people will see that and the really good ones are created to hide a lot of things. I guess for that reason I might be okay but I still hated the idea of going on auditions and having people tell me I wasn't pretty enough or something. My mom said it was interesting and challenging but I saw it start to wear on her.

Grandma wasn't there when I knocked so I went around the back, where she sat sometimes at night to smoke, and it was quiet there, too. That's when I started feeling sick like at night in my bed trying not to breathe or vomit. Because I saw his

Buick sitting there in the sand.

Maybe I have read too many fairy tales. Maybe no one will believe me.

I poked around the house and looked through the windows and after a while I heard their voices and I saw them in this cluttered little storage room piled up with the stuff she sells at the store. Everything looked this glazed brown fluorescent color. When I saw his face I knew something really bad had happened. I remembered the dream I had had and thought about my mom. All of a sudden I was inside that room, I don't really remember how I got there, but

I was standing next to my grandma and I saw she had her shotgun in her hand.

He was saying, Barb, calm down, now, okay. Just calm down. When he saw me his eyes narrowed like dark slashes and I heard a coyote out in the night.

My grandmother looked at me and at him and her mouth was this little line stitched up with wrinkles. She kept looking at him but she said to me, Babe, are you okay?

I said I had heard him yelling at mom and I left. She asked him what happened with Nance and he said they had a little argument, that was

126

all, put down the gun, please, Barb.

Then I just lost it, I saw my grandma maybe start to back down a little and I went ballistic. I started screaming how he had raped me for years and I wanted to kill him and if we didn't he'd kill us. Maybe my mom was already dead.

I don't know what else I said, but I do know that he started laughing at me, this hideous tooth laugh, and I remembered him above me in that bed with his clammy hand on my mouth and his ugly ugly weight and me trying to keep hanging on because I wouldn't let him take my mom away, that was the one thing he

127

could never do and now he had. Then I had the gun and I pulled the trigger. My grandma had taught me how once, without my mom knowing, in case I ever needed to defend myself, she said.

My grandma says that she did it. She says that he came at us and she said to him, I've killed a lot prettier, sweeter innocents than you with this shotgun, meaning the animals when she used to go out hunting, which is a pretty good line and everything, but she didn't do it. It was me.

I have no regrets about him. I don't care about much anymore, really. Only one thing.

Maybe one night I'll be asleep and I'll feel a hand like a dove on my cheekbone and feel her breath cool like peppermints and when I open my eyes my mom will be there like an angel, saying in the softest voice, When you are born it is like a long, long dream. Don't try to wake up. Just go along until it is over. Don't be afraid. You may not know it all the time but I am with you. I am with you.

ROSE

hen Rose White and Rose Red are little, they tell each other, We will never need anyone else ever, we are going to do everything together. It doesn't matter if we never find anyone else. We are complete.

Rose White is smaller and thinner and her hair is like morning sunlight; it breaks easily. Rose Red is faster and stronger and her hair is like raging sunset and could be used to hang jewels around someone's neck. Rose White is quiet and Rose Red talks fast, she is always coming up with ideas—they will go ride the rapids, climb down to the bottom of the canyons, travel to far-off lands where babies wear nothing but flowers and their feet can never touch the floor. Rose Red's voice evokes volcanoes, salt spray, cool tunnels of air, hot plains, redolence, blossoms. Rose White listens and smiles. Yes— worlds, waters, rocks, stars, color so much color. She can see it all when Rose Red speaks. She can see herself balanced precariously on steep precipices or swimming through

134

churning waters — with Rose Red.

Rose Red gives Rose White courage and Rose White gives Rose Red peace. Rose White brushes out the fiery tangle of Rose Red's hair, helps her pick out her dresses, makes her sit down to eat her meals. Rose White makes pumkin soup, salads of melon and mints and edible flowers. She makes dresses out of silk scarves. When Rose Red's heart quickens and her skin flushes like her hair, Rose White listens to her until she is quiet, tells her she is right — the world is a strange mad place, it isn't Rose Red who is mad. Rose Red's world is where she wants to live.

135

When Rose White gets too quiet,
too cold, too deep within herself,
afraid to speak, afraid to be seen,
Rose Red puts a hat on her head,
takes her hand, and brings her out
where it is warm and bright. Even
though they have not traveled far,
with Rose Red it is always an adven-
ture. She knows places to go where
you can dance to live drums, eat
spicy foods with your hands, buy
magic talismans.

One day Rose Red takes Rose
White farther away than they have
been before. They are in the woods
gathering berries — which they eat till
their hands and tongues are purple —

136

burying their faces in the pine needles, practicing bird calls, chasing butter-flies. They climb trees and bathe in a stream and adorn themselves with moss and vines and wildflowers. They lose track of time. Rose Red does because she wants time to be lost and Rose White does because she trusts Rose Red and so forgets to worry. But then it is suddenly night and the trees become hovering spec-ters and the wind is lost ghosts and the owls are mournful phantoms. Rose White is afraid and Rose Red is becoming afraid, not of the night but because she is not sure she can con-sole Rose White this time, or regain her trust. We'll be all right, she says. We have each other. But she knows that, as the night goes on, Rose White is not content with this—she wants to be rescued, she wants someone from the outside who has a light and strength that Rose Red does not have. Rose White is crying and her dress keeps getting caught on branches and her face is scratched and she is cold. Rose Red gives her her sweater but it doesn't help much. Rose White is shivering. She says, How could this have happened? What were we thinking? We've got to get help. This is how girls die. She is sobbing.

Then Rose Red sees the light shining in the trees. To Rose Red the light is like Rose White, it is made for Rose White. Her relief is not for herself—if it wasn't for Rose White, Rose Red would stay out in the forest until dawn, maybe for days and nights, maybe forever, growing wilder and wilder until she is a part of the trees and dirt and darkness— but Rose White is more important to her than all the freedom and all the wildness she desires. She has to raise her voice so that Rose White will stop crying and hear her—There, see the light, there, for you.

They go toward it and when they

see the little cottage they are not afraid, even Rose White is not afraid because the cottage is made of round stones with a thatched roof and a smoking chimney and moss growing on the walls and a carefully tended garden. They go up the little stone path among the hollyhocks, morning glories, the carrots and tomatoes and strawberry vines, and Rose Red knocks on the little green door with the big brass knocker.

No one answers. Rose Red peeks through the lace-curtained window. She sees a room warmed by firelight, a wooden floor, cushions, a small table with a blue-and-white-checked cloth and a milk pitcher full of daisies and honeysuckle. Come on, Rose Red gestures, and she gently pushes the door open.

That is when they see the Bear. Rose White steps back but Rose Red reaches for her hand and they stand very still. The Bear blinks up at them with his flickering fire-lit brown eyes. The tip of his snout quivers. His breathing is labored. He shifts his weight and his front paws sway in the air. His claws are long and sharp. Rose White and Rose Red hold their breath.

He's hurt, Rose Red says. Yes, there is a large wound in the Bear's

141

side. His blood is pooling onto the braid rug. Rose Red moves slowly toward him. It's all right, she says, we won't hurt you. Let me see you.

She kneels down and they look at each other. The Bear smells of forests, smoke, berries. After a long time, Rose Red moves closer. She puts out her hand, palm down. The Bear sniffs it, licks it with his long, rough, pink tongue. Yes, there, it's all right, Rose Red says.

Rose Red goes and fills a basin with water from the well outside. She gives it to the Bear to drink. Rose White takes some berries from her pockets and holds out her hand.

The Bear nuzzles her palm with his damp snout, tickles her as he eats. Rose White rips a piece of cloth from the bottom of her dress. She and Rose Red wash the wound and gently bandage it. The Bear lies back awkwardly, heavily, on the cushions and watches them. That is when Rose White realizes what it is he reminds her of. She can't stop thinking this. She is less surprised by the thought than by the realization that she does not want to share it with the person who has known every single thing about her since the day they were born.

After a while Rose Red and Rose

White fall asleep. In the morning they feed the Bear again and help themselves to bread and honey and cheese, milk and berries. They go out into the woods. Neither of them mentions the idea of going home. They forage for food for the Bear. Roots, nuts, more berries. A little ways from the cottage they find a beehive that someone has been tending, and Rose Red puts on the beekeeper's suit and collects some of the honey to replenish the Bear's supply. They bathe in the stream and wash their dresses, dry them in the sun. When they dress, Rose Red notices that Rose White seems to be taking

144

more care than usual. Her hair is
sunlight in sunlight. Her cheeks are
pink. She makes herself a wreath of
wildflowers. She is wearing the dress
with the torn hem out of which she
made a bandage for the Bear.

Rose Red knows what is happening, a part of her knows. She remem-
bers what she and Rose White used
to say to each other when they were
young. She touches her hair—it feels
coarse. She looks at her freckled
arms and her big strong calves. She
looks at Rose White admiring herself
in the stream, casting white petals
over her reflection.

The Bear is better that night. His

breathing is more regular and he eats more of the food they give him. Rose Red builds a fire in the fireplace. She sees the way the Bear stares at Rose White while she cleans and rebandages his wound. His eyes are full of dark firelight. Full of light and strength. Watching the Bear and Rose White, Rose Red feels the way she felt when she and Rose White first discovered the Bear—she can't breathe, her body seems to have frozen.

Days go by. Rose White and Rose Red spend them in the woods. Rose White's skin is glowing and her body seems to be filling out. Neither

146

ROSE

she nor Rose Red ever talk of leaving.
At night they watch over the Bear.

One night it is especially cold.
Rose Red wakes in the little bed with
the carved headboard painted with
blue hearts and yellow birds. Rose
White is not there. Rose Red goes
into the front room. The Bear is
sleeping by the fireplace where he
always sleeps. His wound has completely healed. His coat gleams. Rose
White is curled up in the curve of his
haunches. Rose Red stops breathing;
she freezes. She knows that what
Rose White told her once would now
be a lie. She goes back to her bed and
stares into the darkness where trans-

147

formations are taking place.

In the morning when Rose Red comes in for breakfast she sees a man sitting with Rose White at the little table with the blue-and-white-checked cloth. He is tall and strong, with a shiny brush of brown hair and fierce spellbinding brown eyes. He is staring at Rose White, whose hair is like the honey sunlight pouring in through the leaded glass window; she has berry-stained lips and hands and is wearing her flower wreath and her dress that is half the size it once was because it has been turned mostly into bandages.

Rose White runs to Rose Red

and kisses her with her berry-stained lips. Rose Red swallows a trickle of salt in her throat and smiles. She says, This is what is supposed to happen, I'm so happy for you.

Rose White wants to tell her, maybe he has a friend, you have to stay with us, things don't have to change that much, but she doesn't say anything. She knows that things have changed. When Rose Red sets out to leave she holds his hand and lets her go.

BONES

I dreamed of being a part of the stories — part of the stories — even terrifying ones, even horror stories — because at least the girls in stories were alive before they died.

My ears were always ringing from the music cranked to pain-pitch in the clubs. Cigarette smoke perfumed my hair, wove into my clothes. I took the occasional drug when it came my way. The more mind-altering the better. I had safe sex with boys I didn't know — usually pretty safe. I felt immortal, which is how you are supposed to feel when you are young, I guess, no matter what anybody older tells you. But I'm not sure I wanted immortality that much then.

I met him at a party that a girl from my work told me about. It was at this house in the hills, a small castle that some movie star had built in the fifties with turrets and balconies and balustrades. People were bringing offerings — bottles of booze and drugs and guitars and drums and paints and canvases. It was the real bohemian scene. I thought that

in it I could become something else,
that I could become an artist, alive.
And everyone else wanted that, too;
they were coming there for him.

Once he'd come into the restaurant late at night and I took his order
but he didn't seem to notice me at
all. I noticed him because of the color
of his hair and goatee. I heard that
he was this big promoter guy, managed bands, owned some clubs and
galleries. A real patron of the arts,
Renaissance man. Derrick Blue they
called him, or just Blue. It was his
house, his party, they were all making
the pilgrimage for him.

It was summer and hot. I was

sweating, worried my makeup would drip off. Raccoon pools of mascara and shadow around my eyes. The air had that grilled smell, meat and gasoline, that it gets in Los Angeles when the temperature soars. It was a little cooler in the house so I went in and sat on this overstuffed antique couch under some giant crimson painting of a girl's face with electric lights for her pupils, and drank my beer and watched everybody. There was a lot of posing going on, a kind of auditioning or something. More and more scantily clad girls kept coming, boys were playing music or drawing the girls or just lying back, smoking.

156

Derrick Blue came out after a
while and he made the rounds —
everybody upped the posing a little
for him. I just watched. Then he
came over and smiled and took my
hand and looked into my eyes and
how hungry I was, in every way.
I was always hungry for food —
blueberry pancakes and root beer
floats and pizza gluey with cheese —
I thought about it all the time. And
other things. I'd sit around dreaming
that the boys I saw at shows or at
work — the boys with silver earrings
and big boots — would tell me I was
beautiful, take me home and feed me
Thai food or omelets and undress me

157

and make love to me all night with the palm trees whispering windsongs about a tortured, gleaming city and the moonlight like flame melting our candle bodies. And then I was hungry for him, this man who seemed to have everything, and to actually be looking at me. I didn't realize why he was looking.

He found out pretty fast that I wasn't from around there, didn't know too many people well, lived alone in a crummy hotel apartment in Koreatown, ate what I could take home from work. He knew how hungry I was. He asked everything as if he really cared and I just stared back at him and answered. He had blue eyes, so blue that they didn't dim next to his blue-dyed hair. Cold beveled eyes. They made the sweat on my temples evaporate and I felt like I was high on coke coke coke when he looked at me.

The crimson girl on the wall behind me, the girl with the open mouth and the bared teeth and the electric eyes, looked like she was smiling—until you looked closely.

Derrick Blue caught my arm as I was leaving—I was pretty drunk by then, the hillside was sliding and the flowers were blurry and glowy like in those 3-D postcards—and it was

159

pretty late, and he said, stay. He said
he wanted to talk to me, we could
stay up all night talking and then
have some breakfast. It was maybe
two or three in the morning but the
air was still hot like burning flowers.
I felt sweat trickle down my ribs
under my T-shirt.

We were all over his house. On
the floor and the couches and tables
and beds. He had music blasting
from speakers everywhere and I let it
take me like when I was at shows,
thrashing around, losing the weight
of who I was, the self-consciousness
and anxiety, to the sound. He said,
You're so tiny, like a doll, you look

160

like you might break. I wanted him to break me. Part of me did. He said, I can make you whatever you want to be. I wanted him to. But what did I want to be? Maybe that was the danger.

The night was blue, like drowning in a cocktail. I tasted it bittersweet and felt the burning of ice on my skin. I reeled through the rooms of antiques and statues and huge-screen TVs and monster stereo systems and icy lights in frosted glass. If you asked me then if I would have died at that moment I might have said yes. What else was there? This was the closest thing to a story I'd ever known. In-

161

side me it felt like nothing.

That night he told all the tales. You know, I am still grateful to him for that. I hadn't heard them since I was little. They made me feel safe. Enchanted. Alive. Charms. He said he had named himself for Bluebeard, if I hadn't guessed. He said it had become a metaphor for his whole life. He took a key from his pocket. I wasn't afraid. I couldn't quite remember the story. I felt the enchantment around us like stepping into a big blue glitter storybook with a little mirror on the cover and princesses dancing inside, dwarves and bears and talking birds. And dying girls.

He said, The key, it had blood on it,
remember? It was a fairy, and she
couldn't get the blood off, no matter
what she did. It gave her away. I
knew that Bluebeard had done
something terrible. I was starting to
remember. When I first heard that
story I couldn't understand it—why
is this a fairy tale? Dead girls in a
chamber, a psychotic killer with blue
hair. I tried to speak but the enchantment had seeped into my mouth like
choking electric blue frosting from a
cake. I looked up at him. I wondered
how he managed it. If anyone came
looking for the women. Not if they
were a bunch of lost girls without

voices or love. No one would have come then.

Part of me wanted to swoon into nothing, but the other women's bones were talking. I didn't see the bones but I knew they were there, under the house. The little runaway bones of skinny, hungry girls who didn't think they were worth much—anything— so they stayed after the party was over and let Derrick Blue tell them his stories. He probably didn't even have to use much force on most of them.

I will rewrite the story of Bluebeard. The girl's brothers don't come to save her on horses, baring

164

swords, full of power and at exactly the right moment. There are no brothers. There is no sister to call out a warning. There is only a slightly feral one-hundred-pound girl with choppy black hair, kohl-smeared eyes, torn jeans, and a pair of boots with steel toes. This girl has a little knife to slash with, a little pocket knife, and she can run. That is one thing about her—she has always been able to run. Fast. Not because she is strong or is running toward something but because she has learned to run away.

I pounded through the house, staggering down the hallways, falling

165

down the steps. It was a hot streaky dawn full of insecticides, exhaust, flowers that could make you sick or fall in love. My battered Impala was still parked there on the side of the road and I opened it and collapsed inside. I wanted to lie down on the shredded seats and sleep and sleep.

But I thought of the bones; I could hear them singing. They needed me to write their song.

BEAST

eauty's father thought that he was through having children. His two daughters were a handful, running around the house, demanding that he look at them, compliment them. He didn't have much energy anymore. He was getting old, much older than his wife. Look at his wrinkles, look at his gray hair. What if he became ill and died before the baby was grown? But his wife convinced him —

There's one more. Please. I feel her. Beauty's father said no; his wife insisted. She won. Soon after giving birth to Beauty, she was the one who got sick and died.

Beauty's father loved his youngest daughter, the child of his old age, more than anything in the world. Maybe too much. After all, it was he who had named her. That was the first clue. It wasn't an easy name to have, no matter what you looked like. It predisposed her sisters to hate her from the beginning.

Not only was the name a bad choice; Beauty's father also picked the forbidden rose to bring to her. But it was necessary. Otherwise how would Beauty have met the Beast?

Beauty's father had to go away on a trip to purchase goods to sell in his store. He asked Beauty's sisters what they wanted, and they listed silk dresses with silver sari trim, pearled camisoles, lace nightgowns, ruby earrings, and French perfume. Beauty, who had her father's love and so didn't feel a need for much else, requested a single rose—she knew it would make him happy. This irritated her sisters to no end. They might even have asked for roses, too, if they had thought of it, and if it would have made their father love them more. But no, it was always Beauty who thought of those things first, making them look foolish and selfish. Well, it was too late. Now they would have their nice gifts, anyway. How could their father deny them? He would have felt too guilty, since they all knew whom he favored.

Beauty's father found the silk dresses with silver trim, the pearled camisoles, lace nightgowns, ruby earrings, and French perfume. He was going to wait until the last minute for the rose so that it would be fresh when he gave it to his daughter. But on the way home Beauty's father lost his way on a deserted road on a cliff between an ocean and a dark wood.

Then he saw a light, a melding rainbow light shining in the trees, and Beauty's father felt compelled to go to it. He walked through the pines and the redwood trees that towered above him. There were a few charred tree trunks blocking the paths; new, young trees grew out of these carcasses. He had read somewhere that when a redwood is burned it will be shocked into sprouting new greens from its roots so that a young tree will grow. Otherwise the baby tree would never have been born.

173

Pine needles and dead leaves slipped under his feet and he sank into dampness, branches catching at his clothes. His heart was beating at the root of his tongue and his hands were clammy but he kept on.

Beauty's father was relieved to come out of the forest. The house he had seen from the road was huge and made of stone. Each window was of stained glass, so that it almost resembled a cathedral. The garden surrounding the house was overflowing with flowering plants bathed in colored lights. The blossoms were the biggest, richest, and most succulent Beauty's father had ever seen. He

174

knew that Beauty would love them.

Beauty's father walked up stone steps through the garden. The plants formed a bower, showering him with droplets of moisture and sweetening the air. He thought he heard music playing—light and tinkling and other-worldly.

The doors of the house opened as if by themselves, and Beauty's father felt the warmth from inside, heard the music more loudly now, saw a glow of light. He walked in.

There was a long hallway lit by torches in sconces in the shapes of outstretched arms. Trees grew up from the floor and out through the

175

ceiling. Flowering vines grew over all
the furniture. There were many low
cushions in soft, luxurious though
somewhat worn fabrics. Everywhere
was a comfortable, warm corner to
curl up in.

Beauty's father smelled delectable
food wafting through the rooms. He
followed the scent to a dining area
with a low table and more cushions.
Torches burned. On the table was a
feast. Platters of steaming, seasoned
meats, vegetables, and grains made
Beauty's father salivate like an animal. There were no utensils but
when he saw the little sign telling
him to Please Eat, he didn't hesitate

176

to voraciously lap everything up.

Afterward, Beauty's father lay back on the cushions. He closed his eyes and fell asleep.

When he woke he began to explore. He came to a courtyard garden where the flowers were even bigger and more lavish than the ones he had seen in front of the house.

That was when Beauty's father noticed the rose. The rose that proved he loved his daughter too much. There was a little sign in front of it that read, Please Do Not Pick the Flowers.

The rose reminded him of his daughter—open, glowing, pink and white, fragrant. Did he know it

177

reminded him of her because it was forbidden? He only knew he had to have it. It looked fresh enough to last for days and he wasn't that far from home—he could keep it in a jar of water.

But when he leaned to pluck it the inevitable happened. Didn't he realize? How often has this been told?

The Beast came out of the shadows, lumbering on his four legs, his four weighty paws; his glossy black coat moving liquidly over his muscular body, his huge, heavy head swaying slightly, the squareness of it, his big jaw to hold his sharp teeth. All of

178

this distracted Beauty's father so much, of course, that he did not look into the Beast's eyes. If he had, he might not have been afraid. Or maybe, more so? The Beast's eyes were the dark, slightly slanted, loving, fierce, hypnotizing eyes of a god.

You take the one thing that you are not allowed to touch? growled the Beast. You have insulted me and my hospitality.

Beauty's father apologized, wondering what had been in the food. What kind of dream was this? And how could he wake up?

The Beast stalked around Beauty's father in circles, like a nightmare, his

179

head slung low between his shoulder blades, the hairs on his back standing up.

Beauty's father tried to explain, mumbled something about his daughter, Beauty, how all she wanted was a rose, he loved her, wasn't thinking, had never seen flowers like that, never seen . . .

After what seemed like a very long time, the Beast told Beauty's father that he could go. On one condition.

This was the part Beauty's father somehow knew. He began to shake his head, no, not that, anything else. The Beast said it was the only way.

Beauty's father must obey, otherwise when he returned home he would become very ill and die.

Beauty's father left the Beast's home, running down the stone corridors where the hands holding torches seemed to reach out to burn him, staggering out the heavy door through the garden that now smelled suffocating, into the dark forest that was now comforting. He saw a faint light at the edge of the sky and knew it would be day soon—he could find someone to take him to the nearest town. He was alive, he had had a terrible dream.

But in his hand was the rose.

181

Beauty's father returned home with the gifts for his daughters. The two older ones weren't particularly impressed—this was because they knew his love for them was not bleeding in the rubies or anywhere else. Only Beauty expressed delight. She kissed his hands, thanking him. His hands that were covered with pale brown spots and thick blue veins. His hands that had comforted and protected her since she was born, a child of his old age whom he thought he would never see grow into womanhood. She knew how precious the rose gift was. It was a sign of his devotion, and, ultimately, a release from it.

A few days after he'd returned home, Beauty's father became ill. Beauty put him to bed where she fed and bathed him. He had glass eyes and parchment lips. His skin burned with a mysterious fever. Beauty asked him what was wrong over and over again. She sensed he was hiding something from her. What was it? Had he been to a doctor and found something? Why wouldn't he go see one now? Beauty's father finally admitted that something strange had happened to him on his trip. He wouldn't say more but one night, in a dream, he spoke out loud about

183

the Beast and the rose, and Beauty
heard. She made him tell her when
he woke up.

After Beauty's father had told her
the story, he regretted it and tried
to say it was just delirium from the
fever. But she was too wise for
that. Besides, secretly, without even
knowing it herself, she had been waiting for a Beast to go to.

Because of this, it was easier than
it might have sounded for Beauty to
go to the Beast. She would not listen
to her father's pleas; she had made
up her mind. It was the first time she
had ever disobeyed him.

Beauty rode along the coast,

marveling at the changing colors of the ocean, the sea lions she saw sleeping on the sand like shifting black rocks, the formations of birds writing poetry in the sky, zebra grazing in a field among some cows and horses. She sang to herself and let the wind tangle her hair. She had never felt so free. This was the right thing, she knew.

But then she got to the wood and saw the house and she became afraid. She had had so little time to feel herself, without the weight of her sisters' jealousy, her father's love. She wanted more wind and sea and zebras. Now she was going into another locked place.

Still, she had made her promise. So she walked through the garden filled with tempting flowers, and through the doors that opened as she approached them, down the hallway lit with torches. She sat on a cushion in front of a low table that was spread with foods she had never seen or even heard of before. There were translucent sweet red and green fruits shaped like hearts, bright gold roasted-tasting grains shaped like stars, huge ruffley purple vegetables and small satiny blue ones. Everything smelled fresh and rich and light, and Beauty found herself

186

stooped over her plate, licking it, like a wild animal. She ate until she was too full to move and then she lay back on the cushions and fell asleep.

When she woke, the candles had burned down to lumpy puddles of wax, and she had been undressed and tucked into a bed made from the cushions. She sat up, holding her arms over her chest. Who had done this? Why hadn't she heard or felt him? Where was he now?

As if in answer the Beast came out from behind a curtain and sat down on his haunches before her, looking at her with those slanted dark eyes. She could not look away.

187

Did you undress me? she asked.

The Beast nodded his huge head. He looked so gentle and kind that she didn't know what to say next. She wanted to stroke his fur and scratch his ears until he cocked his head and rumbled his throat with pleasure. She wanted to get up and run with him through the woods until they fell down weak and panting with exhaustion. She wanted to lie against his warm, heaving side and sleep.

And this was just what happened. For the next few weeks Beauty and her companion never spoke. He knew her thoughts and

188

tried to give her everything she needed. Even more—he seemed to feel her feelings. When she was sad he moaned softly in his sleep, then woke to nuzzle his cool nose against her neck. When she was happy he frisked around her, wagging and wiggling with joy like a pup. They ate together at the low table and ran together through the woods. The Beast showed Beauty secret pathways and how to hear sounds that had once been hidden from her, how to read the scents among the foliage—who had been there, what they desired, where they had gone. When the smells were evil the Beast

189

became wild, baring his teeth, grab-
bing Beauty's dress in his teeth,
practically dragging her back with
him to the house. She was never
afraid, though, not with the Beast
beside her, not with what he had
taught her.

Beauty began to change. Her
hair was always a tangle, she bathed
less often, her skin smelled of the
garden and the forest, she was almost always barefoot—there were
hard calluses on her soles. Her senses
were so sharp that she could smell
and hear things she had never known
existed before. This was the happi-
est she had ever been in her life, if

190

happiness is waking with a start of joy for the day, feeling each moment in every cell of your being, and going to sleep at night with a mind like a clear moonlit sky.

Beauty was never overwhelmed or suffocated by the Beast's love, even though, when she left him alone, even for a short time, he looked as if his heart was literally cracking in half inside his chest. But he understood freedom, her Beast. He understood shackles. He never wanted her to feel chains around her neck as he had once felt them. But now she had become his chain in a strange way, and he knew it.

When Beauty called her father that first night he heard the light and air in her daughter's voice and almost immediately he was better. It was as if the guilt he had carried for so long about his wife's death (had he loved his youngest daughter too much, is that why she died?), the neglect of his other daughters, his blind, panicky obsession with Beauty that had driven him to pick the rose that now imprisoned her—because he had told her about it!—was all gone now.

But after a few weeks, he began to long for her again—just to see her face. He knew he was going to die soon. Please come back home, he begged her. Just for a little while.

Beauty asked the Beast. He lay his heavy, warm, silky head in her lap and gazed up at her. How could he deny her anything? He felt her need to see her father in his own heart as only Beasts can.

So Beauty left him and went home. Her father was startled at how his Beauty had changed. He asked again and again if she was sure she was all right, was the Beast hurting her in any way? No, she reassured him. She was happy. Her sisters were horrified. They thought she looked hideous—what was she doing out

193

there in the woods? Beauty smiled at
them and shook her matted locks
and tried to restrain herself from
licking her hand as if it were a paw.

Beauty sat by her father's side
and held his hand and spoke softly
but all she was thinking about, really,
was her Beast. How they didn't need
words. How ferocious he became if
he ever thought she was in danger.
How gentle he was, licking her nose;
no one in the world could be so gentle. How she had become so different
since she had been with him, so much
stronger—she could run for hours
now—so much more perceptive and
tangled, and how she slept so much

better and ate so much more.

Every night before she went to sleep she sent him messages and received his. This was not hard to do—he had taught her about communicating without words. But each time a message came, Beauty felt his sadness growing deeper, so painful that she wasn't sure which of their emotions she was feeling, his or hers. It was like a sickness and she sent him the message that she would return to him as soon as possible, but not yet, her father still needed her.

After Beauty's father died, she wept. But she also felt a strange sense of relief. The relief frightened her. She went back to her Beast. He was lying by the cold fireplace, with his head down; he was too weak to stand. His eyes were blank, his coat was dull and sparse, his bones stuck out. He looked as if he were dying. Beauty was shocked that she had been so wrong not to see, not to come to him sooner. She was so shocked by his pain that she didn't even notice the biggest change of all that came about when she threw her arms around him and told him again and again that she loved him more than anyone in the world, she would never love anyone else in such a pure, vast way.

Yes, the Beast changed.

He spoke more now, and did not gaze at Beauty in the same intense, almost pained way, as if he were feeling every emotion she felt. He did not sigh in his sleep when she sighed and his stomach didn't growl when hers hurt. He could not read her thoughts anymore, and she could not read his. He seemed a bit more clumsy and guarded and distant, too. They no longer ran through the woods together, although they still walked there sometimes. They quarreled and raised their voices to each other once in a while. Each time, after they quarreled, Beauty bathed,

197

combed the tangles from her hair, and began to wear shoes again for a few days.

Beauty loved him more than anything, her Beast boy, but, secretly, sometimes, she wished that he would have remained a Beast.

ICE

She came that night like every girl's worst fear, dazzling frost star ice queen. Tall and with that long silver blond hair and a flawless face, a perfect body in white crushed velvet and a diamond snowflake tiara. The boys and girls parted to let her through—they had all instantaneously given up on him when they saw her.

I felt almost—relieved. Like that

first night with him but different. Relieved because what I dreaded most in the whole world was going to happen and I wouldn't have to live with it anymore—the fear.

There is the relief of finally not being alone and the relief of being alone when no one can take anything away from you. Here she was, my beautiful fear. Shiny as crystal lace frost.

I loved him the way it feels when you get hot wax on the inside of your wrist and while it's burning, just as sudden, it's a cool thick skin. Like it tastes to eat sweet snow, above the

202

daffodil bulbs — not that I've ever found it, but clean snow that melts to nothing on the heat of your tongue so that you aren't even sure if it was ever there. I loved him like spaniel joy at a scent in the grass — riveted, lost. I loved him so much that it felt as if it had to be taken away from me at any moment, changed — how could something like that be allowed to exist on this earth?

We lived in apartments that faced each other and sometimes I'd look up when I was painting and I'd see him watching me but then he'd look away. I watched him, too, when he was practicing his guitar sometimes. We nodded when we saw each other in the street but we never spoke.

I went to the Mirror one night by myself and when I heard him sing I could feel everything he was feeling. I could feel the throb in the ankle he'd twisted jumping into the pit a couple of nights before, the way the sweat was trickling down his temples, making them itch, the way his throat felt a little bit scratchy and sore and how he wanted to go away from that smoky room, drive out to the lake for some air, how there was something from his childhood that he was trying to forget by singing but

204

how it never quite left him—though
I couldn't quite feel what it was. I
have felt people before; my mom
used to call me an empath. When she
got sick I developed lumps in my
breasts and my hair was falling out
for a while. It only happened with
people I loved, though. Never a
stranger. Never a singing stranger
with golden hair tousled in his face
and deep-set blue eyes and a big
Adam's apple. Maybe my empathy
was just because of him. He could
make you feel things. Maybe every
person in that room was feeling what
he did.

But this was what was strange—

he knew me, too. He gazed down through the smoke and kept looking at me while he sang about the shard of glass in his eye. Trying to melt it away. Tears. But he was dry. When it was over I felt like I'd been kissed for hours all over my body. I could feel my own tears running down my cheeks and neck.

I felt small and stupid-looking and bald when it was over, when I came back to my body and my shorn head. I wanted to go and hide from him. But he found me. He came walking through the crowd and smoke and everyone was trying to talk to him or touch him and he

looked wiped out. He looked like he
had given every single thing and
what could they want from him
now? His eyes looked bigger and
more hollowly set and I could feel his
sore throat and his dry burning
glass-stung eyes. He came up to me
and sat down and he asked right
then if I wanted to get out of there
with him, if I wanted to go get high
or whatever, he had to get out right
now he liked the tattoo of the rose on
the inside of my wrist. He didn't say
anything about recognizing me from
before.

The streets were slick with frost,
my fingers and nose and toes went

numb, my toes knocking against my boots with hammering pain. I didn't care. I watched him light a cigarette, holding it in his hand with the fingerless mittens, cupping the flame, protecting it, handing it to me, lighting another for himself. He said he thought smoking was a primitive reflex to the cold—like building fires. The cold inside, too. Our boots crunched through thin sheets of ice. I thought that if I were still crying my tears would freeze and I could give them to him—icicles to suck on. But he needed warming, to be kissed with the fire of a thousand cigarettes.

We walked for a while and then

he got a cab and we went to his place. That's when he said he hoped I didn't mind, that he'd been watching me through the window, he wasn't a crazy stalker or anything, he just couldn't help it. He said not to take this the wrong way but I reminded him of a sister. He said he believed in that thing about everyone having another half out there, like a twin, that you were supposed to find and that almost no one ever did. We sat in the room that I'd seen through glass for so long, the room with the mattress and the music and the thrift shop lamps and we got high and talked all night. Mostly I did; I told

209

him about my mom and he just listened, but he kept thanking me for
telling him. It was almost as if hear-
ing it was as much a relief for him as
my saying it. We both kept saying
how relieved we felt—relieved, that
was the word we kept using. I was
like an accident victim who's been
rescued, pulled breathing from the
wreckage—until I began to feel
afraid.

All that winter I painted him
with his eyes like moons or his head
crowned with stars or a frozen city
melting in his hands. I had some
ideas of how I was going to paint him
riding on the back of a reindeer, eat-

210

ing snowflakes, holding a swan. He
wrote songs about a girl who was a
storm, a fire, a mirror. My hair grew
out and I started wearing sparkling
light-colored soft soft things I'd
found in thrift shops. I had a fake fur
coat and a pastel sequin shirt and
rhinestones. We got the flu and ate
rice balls and miso soup in the bath-
tub. I gave him vitamin C and echi-
nacea. He felt better. We went to the
Mirror and he always made sure to
find me right after he sang and hold
me so no one else would try to touch
him. He knew I was afraid that
somehow he would be taken away
from me. I never said it but I knew

he knew that was why I cried at
night, sometimes, after we had made
the sheets so hot I was afraid they
would stick to our skin like melted
wax. He told me over and over
again, The songs are for you, you are
the girl in the songs, you are all I
think about when I pull you into the
vortex of our bodies. I never really
believed him. Is that why it happened? Because I never believed a
real love which then felt betrayed?
Or was it because I had sensed
something true all along?

Maybe it happened because when
he was sad I tried to get him to remember. I asked what it was he was

212

trying to forget. I said that for me, pain lessened when you let it out, shared it. He shook his head, slid farther away. Maybe I was just being selfish, wanting to know his secret, whatever it was, the one thing he wouldn't let me have.

Spring came. We planted flowers in our window boxes since we didn't have gardens. One morning when we woke up we saw that the tendrils had twisted together, across the space between our windows.

I painted him with flocks of birds circling, opaled wings spreading out of his back, flowers blooming full burst from his mouth. He wrote

213

songs about a girl who was a fish, a light, a rose. He held me every night, his sweat dripping off onto me, his eyes glazed, my throat aching from the strain of his vocal cords. He said he got so tired. That I was the only thing that could restore him. Boys and girls wanted more than just the songs. They wanted to touch him, they wanted to feel what he was feeling after the songs were over, they wanted him to feel them. I took him home with me. We sat curled in my velvet love seat; he held my wrist, asking questions, and I told him what had happened to me. I tried to get him to tell me what hurt him but

214

then he became even more silent.

He began to have trouble writing songs. He looked blurry to me after he sang. He was fading, I was sure of it. Just this blur of gold light. He said he didn't know what people wanted anymore. After a while I couldn't give him himself back after he sang, no matter what I did. I lay awake at night watching him sleep — his eyelashes tipped with gold, the rise and fall of his chest — thinking, any day now, this can't last. Look at him. He is too perfect. Like an angel carved on a tomb. If you try to keep something so perfect, you get only silent stone.

And then winter again.

That was when she came, my beautiful fear. My fear so beautiful that I almost desired it—her. She was the porn goddess, ice sex, glistening and shiny and perfection. Something you wanted to eat and wear and own and be. Something poisonous delicious forbidden.

She went straight for him and he couldn't fight her and I didn't hate him. I just vanished. With my little less-bald-than-it-had-been head and my fuzzy coat and my big boots against which my numb toes would slam. He didn't find me after the show and I was no longer the storm

216

girl, fish girl, rose girl, mirror. I was nothing and she was everything and he was gone.

Later, he saw the rose tattooed on my wrist, and he said, Why did you get that there? The tattoo he had loved the first night we touched. And I said, I told you, remember? I covered some scars when I tried to cut myself after my mom died and he said, I don't know if I can handle this, and turned away. She had changed him. The ice was in his eye and in his heart, like he had predicted with that song, but now they were deep embedded there, all the pain of the world. Not pain to make

217

you feel for somebody else but pain to make you stop feeling.

I would have ridden on a reindeer or the back of a bird, I would have gone to the North Pole and I would have woven a blanket out of the threads of my body. I would have ripped out my hair and had implanted a wig of long silver blond strands, cut my body and sewn on whole new parts. I would have flayed my skin to find a more perfect whiteness beneath. I would have given him my eyes or my heart so that I could live in him, lying in her arms. At least then I could be close to him. These are the things of stories and I couldn't do any of them. All I could do was go back to my room and pull down the blinds and paint.

I painted every story about stolen deadened boys, nearly devoured by evil queens, revived by loving girls. I painted myself ripping out my hair, cutting off parts of me, sewing on new ones. I painted myself on the back of a reindeer. Fish girl storm girl mirror girl. But sometimes art can't save you. It had before I met him but now it couldn't. I painted myself and my twin melding into one and caten by the ice. I was dying but inside him I lived. What would happen to me if she took his soul forever? He is lying in her burning cold bed watching the video screen. This is how they touch. She's too perfect to be real. He touches himself looking at her. Parts of him are dying and he is blissful. Why did he need to feel things for so long? Look where it got him. Hungry hungry boys and girls who would collect pieces of him if they could to put in their beds, scrapbooks, boxes, put on their plates. A twin who wept almost every night thinking she would lose him. He can't do this to her. It's better this way. Poor insecure little bald girl. Remember walking through the frost? Remember her paintings that he said were how things should really look? The flowers tangling into each other? No, he's forgotten. The Ice Queen is undressing for him again.

I'll make you a god, she said.

That's what I heard. At the Mirror, in the streets. She said, Move in with me. I'll give you any-thing you want. How could he refuse? Me crying on the phone. Or her. And everything. It wasn't much of a choice.

Then he disappeared.

She was alone at the Mirror, surrounded by girls and boys who looked ready to lap her up like walk-ing candy. Where is K.? they asked.

She just smiled. So pretty it could blind you. Snowflakes in the sun. Rumors started that he was dead. OD'd. Gun to the skull. She was a killer, you could see it. Someone should go check it out.

But the boys and girls were being fed on her. She started performing for them. They forgot about him.

I'd stare into his dark, empty apartment and see him in the window playing his guitar, dancing around like a puppet with his hair in his face. My beautiful boy. He'd stop, look up, shake away his hair, look across at me with his shadowy eyes. But he wasn't there at all.

A bird landed on my flower box. I asked it had it seen him? The bird said, Ask the flowers. All the ones he and I had planted had died. I walked down by the lake where we used to go. Some roses were struggling up. I asked them. They said they'd been under the ground and he wasn't there. They said I should go to see her.

She lived in a house high above the city and ice was on the ground. Everywhere else it had started to melt. The numb pain came back in my toes and fingers. I walked through the iron gates, up the icy path among the snow-covered trees, over the threshold of the white palace. The floors were cold marble and echoing. Everything was white. The chill was so harsh that I could see my breath, even inside. I went looking for him.

Up white marble stairs into a white marble room decorated with giant crystal snowflakes hanging from the ceiling, catching-refracting the light. He lay sleeping at her feet in a little lump. He was barefoot and his feet looked so cold. The blue veins stood out, vulnerable. I wanted to warm his feet in my armpits but I was cold too. She was even more beautiful than I remembered her. I thought that I had made a mistake. There was no way he could love me after seeing her even just once.

But at least I could touch him again, wake him, something. See if he was still alive inside. Then I'd leave.

She said I really shouldn't come barging in like that, didn't I know he didn't want me anymore? She touched her hair and light leaped off of it like diamonds. She touched her throat and I felt mine close with fear.

I remembered how love is supposed to break evil spells. Only if you love purely. I understood how he

had come to her. He wanted something that could make him forget.
There was something bad enough
inside him that he had to forget
and I couldn't help him. I always
wanted to remember, wanted him
to remember.

But now I thought that if he
opened his eyes I would leave, never
come back to bother him again. I just
had to see if he was all right. Maybe
I could tell him that I understood
about forgetting.

I knelt beside him and put my
hands on his cheekbones. His neck
was limp. I breathed on his face,
whispering his name. My breath

made a cloud and it melted the icicles
on his eyelashes. I said, Come back
here. I just want to see if you're okay.
Then I'll leave if you want. I promise,
I'll leave.

She was watching us, amused, I
think. She stood up and stretched lan-
guidly and slipped off her white satin
gown and waited there naked, burning white and not shivering at all in
the chill air. She was so beautiful that
I thought I had really gone mad this
time, even trying to get him to look
at me.

My tears were so hot that they
didn't freeze on my cheeks. They
poured off of me onto him. They

227

splashed on his upturned face. They poured over his eyelids, dripped into his eyes, seeped into him. I wanted them to wash away the particles of glass.

He looked up at me. He seemed to have shrunken, gotten even paler. He said my name. I wanted to drag him away, covering his eyes, but instead I let him see her there, behind us. Naked and glistening. He stared and I could feel his palm start to sweat, his heart beat fast like it was going to jump into her. I wanted to die, then. I wanted to destroy the body I was trapped in, become what she was, no matter what it took.

228

No matter how much mutilation or pain. But he looked away, at me. He pulled my face down and pressed my lips against his like he was almost trying to suffocate us both.

Once he and I were children, before this happened.

Acknowledgments

I would like to thank my mother, Gilda Block, for her endless nurturing, and my brother, Gregg Marx, for his strength. My editor, Joanna Cotler, has made my dream a reality once again by guiding me with her profound warmth and wisdom. I will always be thankful to Charlotte Zolotow, who was the first editor to take a chance on me and open the doors to a whole new life. And Michael Cart for years of professional support and personal understanding.

I would also like to thank my agents, Lydia Wills and Angela Cheng; and everyone at Harper, including the wonderful Bill Morris, Alicia Mikles, Andrea Pappenheimer, Justin Chanda, Jessica Shulsinger, Ginee Seo, Virginia Anagnos, and Kim Bouchard.

My deepest appreciation to the brilliantly talented Suza Scalora for transforming my books forever with her stunning, enchanted cover art.

My friends who have given me so much understanding and inspiration are too many to be named here, but I would especially like to express gratitude to Tracey Porter, Elana Roston, Elise Cannon, and Hillary Carlip for their kindness, faith, and visions.

Special thanks to Kerry Slattery and her staff at Skylight Books for such an enthusiastic and personalized approach to bookselling.

Finally, I want to send my thanks to all my readers who have shared their joys and pain with me in letters that I treasure.